Crossroads of the Never: Book 1

DANE CLARK COLLINS

Cover art by:
Michael Bielaczyc

Copyright © 2015 Dane Clark Collins
All rights reserved.

ALSO BY
LONE WANDERER ENTERTAINMENT

The Elves of Uteria
The Tomb of Kochun
The Goblins of Kaelnor Forest

FOLLOW DANE CLARK COLLINS

Website: www.daneclarkcollins.com
Amazon: www.amazon.com/author/daneclarkcollins
Goodreads: www.goodreads.com/danecollins
Twitter: www.twitter.com/dane_collins

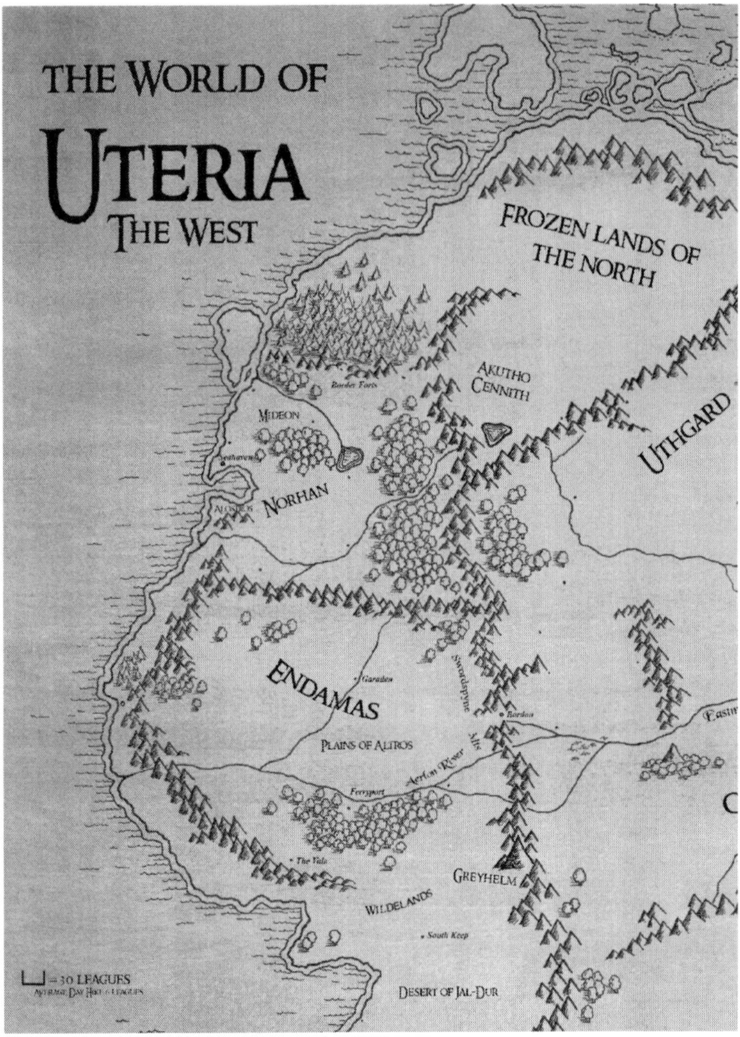
THE WORLD OF
UTERIA
THE WEST
FROZEN LANDS OF THE NORTH
Border Forts
AKUTHO CENNITH
MIDEON
NORHAN
UTHGARD
ENDAMAS
Garadon
Swordspyne Alts
Bordon
PLAINS OF ALTROS
Aerlon River
Ferryport
The Vale
GREYHELM
WILDELANDS
South Keep
DESERT OF JAL-DUR
= 30 LEAGUES

CROSSROADS OF THE NEVER: BOOK 1

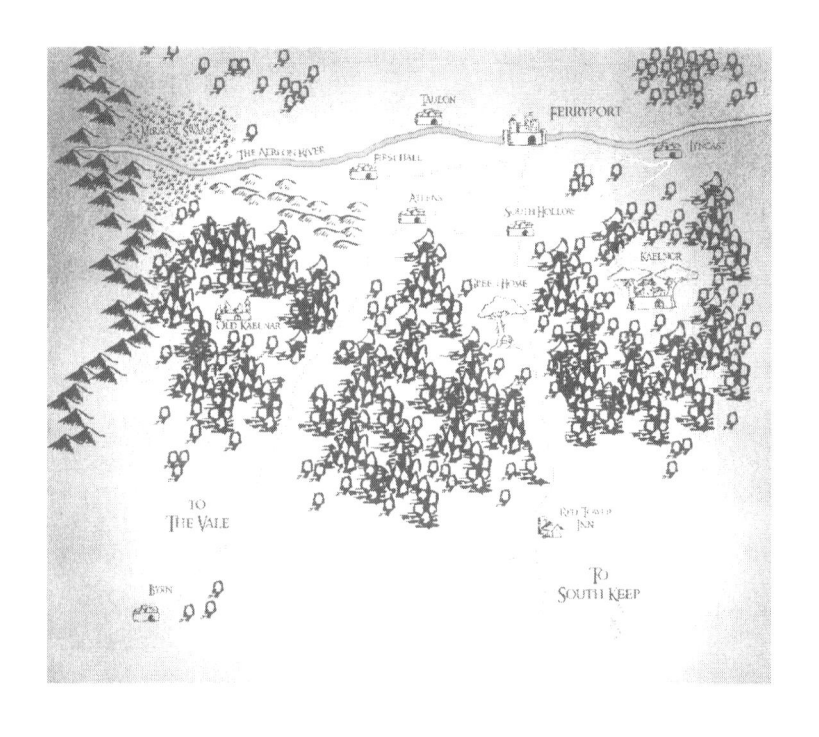

ACKNOWLEDGMENTS

Without the indispensable help of Michael Bielaczyc, this book would not have been possible. Not only is this story based on a world he conceived, but without his consistent encouragement, I might have been defeated by doubt at many steps along the way.

PREFACE

The mood in the tavern was raucous and quickly becoming volatile, and Toryn could sense it.

By the gods, he put them in this state. This was his favorite game, riling crowds and keeping them just on the edge of bursting into chaos, but only barely—walking that needle-sharp line with skill and delicacy. Only twice had he fully lost a crowd, and had fled into the night as the place was destroyed in the violence he left behind. But those were his early days, when he was still practicing. Not any more. If there was one thing Toryn could do well, it was working a crowd.

It wasn't just a game, of course. The challenge was what kept him focused, and kept it fun, but this was hardly the purpose. What Toryn understood was that when people were riled nearly to the point of losing themselves in yelling, fighting, stripping, or just dancing without care, then they thought little of investing their hard-earned coins to keep the mayhem alive. It delivered to them a sense of freedom and adventure their daily lives rarely afforded, so once they were in the frenzied state so artfully crafted by Toryn's ministrations, they would invest anything to keep the festivities alive throughout the night.

And if the morning brought a pounding head, a humiliating story, or even a lumpy, beaten face, it also brought a smile. Nobody would begrudge the entertainer who had invoked such primal revelry.

Every crowd was different, of course, and Toryn would first feel his way through the initial mood. The night was never approached in quite the same way, but there were a few consistencies that constituted Toryn's ritual for laying the groundwork. Most important were the opening stages: watch, then listen, then talk—then the fun could begin. Watching would allow him to assess the body language of the crowd, which was of critical importance. Listening would tell him what was on the people's minds. Talking would begin to shift those minds toward the moods he set out to craft. Then, and only then, when he was confident that he was in tune with the crowd, would he begin the night's entertainment.

Sometimes he would begin with a round of drinks for all, on him. This was a small investment for the windfall he would receive by the end of the night. It would endear him to the crowd, would make them feel obliged to stay for a while, and would set in motion the tumultuous tide. He did not depend on intoxication to work his magic, but it could be a valuable tool when employed with care.

He would begin his performance with a carefully selected set of songs, based on the region, culture, and the current mood. The best songs to begin with were usually the ones that allowed people to sing along. This meant the opening song needed to be familiar to his particular crowd, or simple enough to learn after a single round, and it needed to meld with the room's atmosphere. In a room of men fresh from battle, the music might begin with a somber homage to the fallen, then transition into a rambunctious victory anthem. Once he had them hooked, Toryn had much greater flexibility, because the crowd would follow him eagerly. In degrees, he could guide them slowly in any direction, so long as each transition was subtle. Sometimes, he would surprise even himself by singing the songs of the warriors' enemies, just to see if they would join him in honoring the opponents who had so bravely faced them in battle. And they would. Once, the morning following one such experiment, those men had awoken with a new respect for their enemies, and had marched to the neighboring town to request a peaceful resolution to their conflict. Such was the power of Toryn's craft.

This night, however, Toryn had a different objective. He had a very particular story to tell, and he intended for this audience to pay close attention. In fact, this was a story still unfolding, and the current chapter of the story would end with tonight's telling. He did not yet know what the next chapter would bring, but this was the night on which he would face his future.

So far, the night had been much like any other: a rowdy crowd on the verge of madness, kept barely under control by Toryn's skillful direction, using song and wit. But now, Toryn's song began to slow. Subtly. Not enough for anyone to notice, but they could feel it. Their bodies responded. A few people sat down. He slowed the tempo some more, lowering the timbre of his voice, and some of the yelling began to quiet. Several pairs of eyes took on a markedly introspective expression. As the song wound down just a bit more, one man who had been just on the cusp of a fight minutes ago sat and stared thoughtfully into his beer.

The song ended, and Toryn began a droning, hypnotic tune on his lyre. The bartender had stopped serving drinks, and now mindlessly shined the same spot on the counter, staring at the towel as it wiped back and forth, back and forth. Finally, the man set the cloth down and sat on the tall stool behind the counter. No one complained. The room was silent. Toryn quietly set his lyre beside him. He brushed his hands through his sandy hair and leaned slightly forward in his chair, framed by the light of the fire that burned brightly in the hearth behind him. He looked into each pair of eyes, one by one, and they all stared back attentively. The story began.

CHAPTER 1

All storytellers must struggle with beginnings.

If I were to ask you to tell me your story, where would you begin? When you were propelled into the tender warmth of your mother's womb? When you were heaved from your mother and first gazed upon the harsh light of the world? Or would the story not begin until your life found meaning?

Let's assume you have no interest in hearing tales of my toddling years, my struggles to talk, and my years of difficulty in finding my place in the social order of my strange and reclusive family. I'll even skip those vivid memories of hunting boars with my father's bow, for although this was both formative and eventful—not to mention dangerous and often exciting—it is not where this story begins.

No, I suppose this story begins with the death of my parents and my subsequent adoption by the greatest, most tragic man I have ever known.

Ehrin Sutton was a traveling entertainer with a great passion for musical performance. He reveled in performing the sorts of music that could move a listener, propelling the mind into strange, elusive states. The sounds he wove dug deep into a person's soul, and entire audiences would find themselves entranced by the exotic worlds he invoked with sound. Truth be told, he was not a great lutist or singer, and he knew it, but there was something otherworldly and mystifying about his playing. Even when he played a familiar tune, such as The Watcher Watched Over the Wailers, there was something different—something subtle and haunting that you couldn't quite put into words—and people would find themselves mesmerized. In Ehrin's hands, even the most familiar chorus could draw one through a vertiginous array of alien worlds.

It was for his lack of finesse, however, along with his unfortunate appearance, that he struggled greatly to make a living with his craft. No patrons would have him, and even the rougher taverns were reluctant to pay him. And so he spent the majority of his time traveling great distances from town to town, playing for passersby in the hopes they would be pleased enough to toss him the occasional pittance so that he might stave off starvation for another night. It was an unglamorous life, indeed. But this never tarnished his wonderful love for life, so long as he had an instrument to play. And on those occasions when he would find himself without an instrument, he had his voice. And when he lost even his voice from time to time, he had his imagination and the ability to beg and to smile. Rarely was Ehrin without his smile.

***

It was during the winter of my ninth cycle in the small farming community of Poneroy, outside the walls of Ferryport, that the creatures we now call the Fey began to appear. When several reported sightings of these unknown creatures came in from the forests, our first reaction was curiosity. The first creatures we saw appeared strange, but harmless. Some even considered that we might take them in as pets. But they weren't harmless, and they weren't pets. They began killing our beasts, and we grew frightened. The creatures were both stealthy and ferocious, and there was little we could do to impede the infestation. Soon, there was very little left to eat. Finally, the inevitable happened: a townsperson found small bits of a child who had wandered too far from home, and had been dragged into the forest and consumed.

"These creatures are demons," it was declared, "come from the underworld to punish us for some crime against the gods." This came from our righteous mayor, Sanrin Delorif, who had begun a zealous investigation of the supernatural components of our infestation, and had called a village meeting to reveal that the only possible source of our woes was a malignancy from within—a tumor that must be discovered and excised. Evil wears many disguises, he exhorted, and not even our friends and neighbors should be fully trusted.

Children, then, were forbidden from wandering outside alone, and everyone else sequestered themselves in the relative safety of their homes from gloaming to daybreak. My parents, alone, refused to be crippled by fright. Sure, they kept me inside at night to be safe, but they held to their composure while the neighbors succumbed to terror and began looking for scapegoats. Accusations were made, and old rivalries were reignited. Fights erupted, and the magistrate barely kept the community from falling into utter chaos.

When the village council, at the behest of Mayor Delorif, launched an official investigation to seek out those responsible for inviting this disaster upon us, my father refused to take part. So when the fingers began pointing, to whom do you think they pointed? Behind those fingers were men and women driven by the madness of fear, but there was also greed, for the farms were suffering, and the farmers sought recompense—and my father owned a desirable, if small, piece of land.

Fortunately, for a time, the townsfolk were cowards. My father was not a farmer, but a hunter who lived among the farms because of its proximity to the wild woods beyond. As a seasoned hunter, he was quite adept with his bow and his knife. Each morning, he would trek into the woods, and the people would watch from behind their windows, their visages twisted in contemptuous sneers. When he would glance their way, of course, their eyes would fall and their expressions would become vacant. And so life continued, for a time, with our family keeping to ourselves, and the town talking, but never acting.

My father was scared for me, I know, but had resolved not to let me see his fear. I overheard him some nights, crying out in his sleep. One night, after one of his episodes, I listened at my parents' door as they discussed his nightmares. He said he had dreamed of me being executed by the townsfolk, and then thrown in pieces to the demons as an offering, in hopes that they might move on and find game elsewhere. He said that it was his guilt infecting his dreams, though I could not imagine why, for he was a good man, and a great father. Knowing that my father was afraid made me afraid. I realized then that he had pretended calm in order to soothe my fears. This, I understand now, is what a strong parent does. So frightened or not, I resolved to follow his lead and wore a brave mask over my fear, so he never learned that I knew of his nightmares.

One night, the demons descended upon our town in a most vicious attack, leaving behind the corpses of half a dozen beasts as well as two good men, all devoured damn near to the bone, blood and bits of entrails scattered from where the demons had wrestled with the meat, as one might see two hounds wrestle a bit of rope.

It was Ehrin's misfortune that he wandered into town at the height of our community's terror. He was fortunate, however, to have first encountered my father, who was returning from a hunting expedition. A storm was approaching overhead, and Ehrin—ignorant of our village's sore state of affairs—asked if he might wait out the rain in our home in exchange for song and story. My father warned him that it was the wrong time for outsiders, and directed him toward the inner city, but poor Ehrin had already tried his luck in the city. Even there, he explained, the people were far too afraid to appreciate his arts. He had found himself broke, hungry, and without a place to stay.

So my father invited him to our home. Ehrin sat with us for dinner and enjoyed a healthy meal of meats and vegetables—his first, it seemed, in some time. We were not well off, and the demons had killed or chased out much of the game from the forest, but my father was not one to leave someone hungry.

I remember that meal, my last with my family, with as much clarity as the steak and beans I ate this evening. It's interesting, the details you can you remember from just before those moments that change your life. I remember the crust of the bread, just barely toasted, crumbling on my lips and tongue. I remember the smell of the goat cheese, and the texture of the peppered venison, only lightly cooked but heavily seared. I remember the silence around the table as we all ate our food. I remember being thankful that the crackling of the fire provided some sound to mask our chewing.

Ehrin was the last to finish his supper, and just as he was pushing his spoon into his mouth for his final bite, the sound of approaching hooves could be heard outside. The villagers had arrived. Their horses whinnied as they were navigated around the deep puddles left by the dying rain. Then we heard the shouts. My father, with a nod of resignation, rose from his chair and walked to the door.

I can remember how my father looked as he stepped outside into the pink glow of the setting sun, his back straight and head held high. I wasn't aware of the danger he faced at the time, but I'm certain he knew.

I saw nothing, as my mother and our guest held me back, but I could hear their voices.

Reluctance and resolve seemed to grapple in Sanrin's deep, growling voice. "You, your family, and your guest are going to have to come with us, Jass. We're arresting you on suspicion of consorting with the Darkness that brought upon us those creatures from the underworld. How do you want to plea? Before you answer me, Jass, understand that the only way to save your life is to confess, so that we can guide your soul back to the Light. You've been a friend to this town, so I'm giving you this one last chance. I won't be so kind if you refuse my offer."

"I'd like to know how I've become a suspect, Sanrin. You've known me for sixteen years. Have I ever done you wrong? Have I ever done any of you wrong?"

"You always were an outsider, Jass. You walk

among us, but you're not one of us. Now look at you, well fed while the rest of us are hungry, our food taken by those demons! Those demons devour our livestock while you always come back from your hunts with food—from the very forests from which those demons sprung."

There was truth in these words, but that was because my father was better at hunting than the farmers were at protecting their farms. Still, I've come to find this principle consistent in humanity: one who suffers needs someone to blame.

My father's voice remained composed, in stark contrast to Sanrin's conflicted paranoia. "My family has suffered also, Sanrin. You know this. What is your evidence? If you can produce evidence, I'll come with you. Otherwise, please be off."

"We have evidence, Jass. First, you show no concern for the rest of us. When we spoke of trials, you departed, deriding us for wanting to protect ourselves and our families. Of all the councilmen, only you turned your back on us. Only you refuse to do whatever it takes to rid our lands of this vermin.

"Second, while many of us go hungry this evening, you take in a vagrant and feed him. My own child saw him—a dirty and vile looking man, clearly up to no good, with a fiddle on his back. Came wandering in from the forest, he did. My boy followed him, and he says that you spoke with him real familiar-like before leading him back to your home. Soon after, smoke started pouring from your chimney, like you were cooking a feast.

"Third, the gods have sent me omens. Just before the demons came, I began having dreams, and those dreams have persisted every night since. I've dreamed of you, Jass, performing dark sacrifices to summon vile demons through a gateway of shadow. You dance with the demons around a bonfire built with your offerings, and just outside the light of the fire stands a mysterious man with a fiddle strapped to his back. At first, I thought them just odd dreams, but then came the demons, and I began to wonder. Still, I gave you the benefit of the doubt, and then you turned your back on us. I still refused to believe, against my better judgment, and good people died. Now, here you are with that musician. Let me ask you, Jass, does the man carry with him a fiddle?"

There was silence for several uncomfortable moments.

"And finally, Jass, there's the question I've wanted to ask you for years. What happened out in the woods the night your son was born? The midwife swears Renoira was to have twins, and that she would likely not survive the birth for complications. The two of you disappeared, and next morning, you came sneaking back, Renoira healthy as can be, one child in tow. What happened that night, Jass?"

My father did not answer, but merely stood his ground.

"Now come with us. Confess and turn over the man you got with you, so that we might end this plague on our lands."

"I'll do no such thing, Sanrin. I'm going to go inside he house and retire for the evening, and I would appreciate if you would leave my family alone. When you've come to your senses, come talk to me and we'll sort this thing out. But not tonight."

My father then strode calmly inside and closed the door behind him. As soon as the door was sealed shut, the mask of calm evaporated.

"Toryn, you need to run and hide, somewhere away from the house!" Outside, the sound of hooves moved in circles around the house. "They're surrounding us. Toryn, you have to go. I'm going to distract them, and I want you to slip out the back door and into the woods. Climb a tree, because they might come looking for you, and they will find you if you're not well hidden. I've seen men riled up into this sort of a frenzy before. Terrified, looking for someone to blame. Right now, I'm afraid that's us."

The stranger looked resolved, and interjected then, "My arrival seems to have brought this upon your house. Please, don't do this on my account. I'll turn myself over to them. You were kind to me, and you're good people. I can't let this happen to your family."

"Nonsense, you did nothing but accept a meal from a stranger. Had you not appeared, they would still be here—if not tonight, then soon enough. And turning yourself over won't save a one of us."

"I have some crude skill with a bow, then. Let me take the one I see hanging on the wall and protect your son the best I can. I also can hide in a tree, and I hope we can lose them that way. But if we're found, I may have a better chance of keeping the boy safe than he would on his own."

My father nodded his thanks and turned to my mother. He put his hands on her shoulders, and tears formed as they looked into one another's eyes. There was an understanding between them. A somber, resigned acceptance. They nodded subtly to one another, and without further ceremony, my father disappeared out the front door.

The next moments were a blur of motion. I was pulled by my shirt through the back door by a strong hand, and found myself, alongside Ehrin, racing into the woods. Only once did I slow to look back, but before I could, Ehrin grabbed me violently and propelled me forward. We ran for at least a league before coming to a river and finally stopping for a moment. The sky was now dark, but the red moon shone brightly, casting a soft crimson glow over the land.

Ehrin spoke sternly, but kindly. "We'll talk this over soon, but right now there's no time. I'm sorry, Toryn, I really am, but right now I just need you to do what I say. We're going to cross the river, and I need you to submerge yourself completely. You smell of our dinner. I want you to scrub your body the best you can. Use sand from the riverbed. Scrub every inch of your skin and your clothes, and do it quickly.

"We're going to walk downstream in a shallow portion of the river for a while. I don't know if they have hounds, but we're not going to take any chances. Once we're well away from this spot, we'll leave the river, back on this side. They'll believe we've crossed.

"Then we'll walk another half-mile before climbing a tree with a good, solid bough. And there, we'll stay the night.

"I believe we have a good chance of avoiding the men if we do this, but still, we must be vigilant. The forests aren't safe. Perhaps your father didn't bring those creatures to your lands, but they're here nonetheless, living in these woods. So we'll climb high, we'll take watches through the night, and we won't come down until the sun has climbed back into the sky."

"But when will we…"

"I said we'll talk soon. First, we do what I said. Let's go, now."

Without another word, he was submerged in the river, and I followed close behind him.

CHAPTER 2

We found our tree and began to climb. We had heard sounds behind us, distant but distinct, so we rushed to the first branch we found that was large enough to support us. It wasn't until we were in the tree that we noticed the branch was already occupied. A maulkbird stood by its nest between its brood and us, feathers splayed around its head as warning that it was about to attack. It screamed a harsh, guttural screech, and we began to panic. "Ssh…" I remember saying ridiculously. Of course, the bird did not understand "ssh" and continued its squawking. Ehrin reached for it and it sliced his hand with its beak and croaked louder. The little ones, sensing their mother's fear, began an escalating chorus of chirrups.

Ehrin's hand darted forward, grasping the massive red bird around its neck, and twisted. With a crunch, the squawking stopped, and the creature's carcass fell to the ground. Then he overturned the nest, and all of the little ones plummeted to the ground below. The sudden silence was startling.

Tears welled in my eyes, and I glared at Ehrin, only to find his own eyes welling with tears. Looking back, I know how agonizing that must have been to him. Ehrin was a peaceful and selfless man, without the least inclination for violence. He did what he had to in order to save me. But at that moment, I did not yet know him. I was angry, and I was scared, and I wanted to blame him for this entire disaster.

As we lay prone on the bough of the giant oak, no breeze came to stir the leaves, as if the forest had bated its breath. In the perfect silence, we could hear searchers in the distance as they whistled and barked their frustrations at disobeying hounds.

Ehrin's plan had been a good one, and the searchers never found us. It was not long ere the distant sounds of man and hound waned, and we were left alone to our quiet refuge.

After some time had passed, I finally drew the courage to break the silence. "They've gone. I have to go home."

"I'm sorry, boy, but you can't. Not yet."

"I've had time to think, you know. My parents are in danger, and you left them. You were saving yourself. You escaped with me while my parents stayed behind."

He was silent for a time, then said gravely, "I certainly don't feel courageous. Mayhap I could have stayed behind and distracted those men while your folks got away with you. But your father strikes me as a stubborn man, and there was no time for argument. Besides that, it's doubtful it'd worked. That man—that mayor of yours—he had his sights set on your father. Had for some time, by the sound of it."

I knew the truth of what he said, so I dropped it. I could sometimes be an impetuous child, but my father had taught me that when my passions got the better of me, to just stop talking and think on it. So I pulled myself together, and I waited. And finally, lulled by the dulcet dribble of the lazy river, I slept.

***

I awoke to the sound of a baby's whimpering. For a moment, I thought I was dreaming, but as the fog of sleep cleared, the sound did not abate, and I realized it was coming from below. I began to sit up when Ehrin's forearm crossed my chest and held me still. His face moved to inches in front of mine, eyes wild with fright, and he held a crooked finger to his lips. I bit my tongue and forced myself not to make a sound.

I nodded, and Ehrin released me. I turned my head just enough to look down. On the ground, by the base of the tree, there sat an infant, naked and covered with dirt and grime. He played with three bird skulls—the newborn maulkbirds from the nest Ehrin had overturned—and was attempting to stack them on top of a larger fourth. His mood altered in sudden shifts between childish glee and infantile frustration at his own lack of coordination each time the skulls fell. Finally, an exultant squeal escaped his lips as the third skull successfully rested on top, creating a tiny, crooked pyramid. The boy clapped and laughed with glee…until, as one skull was stacked unevenly, the structure collapsed, and the baby began to cry in frustration. He picked up one of the skulls and threw it against the base of the tree.

Despite my horror at this sight, my first instinct was to jump down—to take the carcasses away from the baby, clean the blood from his hands, pick him up, and seek out his parents. Clearly, this baby had been lost or abandoned, though how it could have been lost so far out into the woods was beyond imagining.

I began to move, but Ehrin grabbed me again, more tightly this time. With stern eyes locked on mine, he shook his head and put his fingers over his lips. I was confused, but something felt wrong about this, so I followed his instructions and remained silent. After a moment, I returned my gaze to the baby—and was terrified to find the baby looking straight up at me. I cannot describe the deep foreboding that seized my soul at that moment, but I found suddenly that I was unable to breathe, my throat constricted with terror. I saw now that there was an otherworldly intelligence behind those eyes. Worse, what I had thought was grime now looked more like rot. This, I understood, was no baby. As he stared at me, his moldering body jiggled with sinister laughter.

He reached his arms toward me, and I was overcome with confusion. He was just a baby now, wanting to be held in someone's arms, and I chastised myself for my paranoid hallucinations. My fear eased, and I inched toward the trunk of the tree, but Ehrin gripped my shirt and held me still. Noticing my sudden hesitation, the laughter came to an abrupt stop, and the little face turned sour. Again, the rot became apparent, and it seemed that I was looking at the decayed corpse of a baby, inhabited by some demonic force. Its mouth opened wide—wider than any human baby's possibly could—and an eldritch howl filled the air, vibrating the tree branch with its force. I was racked with pain of a sort I had never experienced in either intensity or kind. I felt as if my soul was being ripped from my body. The world around me warped and twisted before my eyes. The entire structure of existence had become incongruous, as if I were being severed from reality and pulled into a world that could not possibly exist. I was possessed by the deepest terror I have ever known, and believed then that I was being cast into a hell from which I might never escape. Dizzy and disoriented, I could no longer tell which direction was up. I managed, however, to cling to one solitary connection with reality: the understanding that if I fell from this branch, I would be at the mercy of that child-thing. And so I reached out my arms and clung to whatever was around me, and I clutched it to my chest. No matter how confused I became, I merely held on and refused to let go. I felt myself weakening, and considered that I might be slipping away into the coldness of death, but still I clung with all I had.

Finally, after an amount of time I could not possibly guess, but that felt a lifetime, the roaring ceased. Reality, bit by bit, began to return. The trees slowly coalesced back into the shapes I was familiar with. My mind returned, and I found that I was clutching not only to the tree branch, but had also grabbed onto Ehrin's arm in the process. I had his forearm pinned to the branch while his body dangled.

Slowly, I saw clarity come back to his eyes, which now focused on me. As recognition returned, he looked down to find the baby staring up hungrily, mouth gaping and slavering. Ehrin wasted no time in grabbing the branch and climbing back up.

"Thank you, Toryn." We were both breathing heavily and speaking came with difficulty. Still, he repeated, "Thank you."

The experience had drained us both, and we soon lost consciousness. This time, it was to the natural world of dreams that we slipped. When we awoke, the sun had arisen, and the infant was gone.

***

It was a full two days before we emerged from the forest and onto Forest Way. Farmers' and merchants' wagons creaked by on their way to trade with the neighboring towns. We cleaned ourselves up the best we could and stepped out onto the road and into the open sunlight. It felt like emerging from a long dream into a world I had almost forgotten.

I recall a dizzying moment of contemplation as the familiar but suddenly alien world of mundane human interaction came crashing back into my consciousness. We had spent two days sneaking around for fear of demonic forces in secluded necks of the woods and I found it maddening, after our experiences, to hear groups of passing travelers argue in earnest over the most trivial of banalities. For example, a father and son argued over which of them deserved the most credit for repairing their cart. To me, these things now took on such a level of inconsequentiality as to render them utterly absurd and farcical. I found myself laughing at the parade of comedies before me, and looked over to find Ehrin doing the same.

It struck me as quite strange to watch these people go about their daily business, most looking utterly bored as they sat motionless in their seats, keeping weary eyes locked on the road ahead. Many of these people had been, I realized, in this same state of apathetic boredom at the exact same moments that Ehrin and I had been fleeing for our lives in a danger-ridden forest, cast adrift in a shadowy world, surrounded by spectral creatures recently surfaced from the dusky depths of our collective nightmares. For these people, these had been but normal days, each day dissolving into the forgotten seas of more such routine days of the past. I swore that I would make every day distinctive and new, and would never let myself succumb to the tedium I saw in the eyes of those passersby. My success in this promise to myself has varied, but I try.

I was intent on heading directly back to Ferryport, sure that my father had worked out this misunderstanding by now, but Ehrin insisted that we walk to Lyncast first and ask around for any news. It would be safer there, he said, because no one would know either of us. If my father were to come looking for me, he said reassuringly, he would look in the direction of South Hollow first, and would pass through Lyncast on the way.

Once in Lyncast, I became restless, as we seemed to make no progress. It was unbearable for me to watch the sun pass overhead and to be no closer to getting home. Ehrin, given that we had just run from a group of lawmen, did not want to draw undue attention. He wanted to first try listening in on people's conversations, then perhaps talk to some folks, but without asking questions. His fear was that asking too many pointed questions might raise suspicions. But people in Lyncast did not seem particularly talkative that day, so our time was wasted.

I told him that I wasn't going to wait around all day while he stood around doing nothing. I was going to see if my parents were all right, and I was leaving at that moment, with or without him.

"Okay," he said. "You're right. This isn't working. But we can't be reckless. Come with me into this tavern. Let me order a whiskey for myself and some water for you. We're just passing through. We're not here for information; I'm just making conversation with the locals while I drink my whiskey. Do not ask any questions. I want, at least, to try to lead into it naturally. But I promise you, I won't waste time. I'll ask about Poneroy, and if there's no news, we'll head back. Carefully. Is that fair?" I nodded sullenly, and we walked into Nad Wailen's Tavern.

The place was filthy. All taverns seemed dirty to me, as a child—my apologies to the owner of this fine establishment; you're clearly the exception—but Nad Wailen's Tavern truly was filthy. Crusty. We kicked up dust as we crossed the floor. The tables were sticky with spilled beer that had not been cleaned. The place reeked of dried beer, rat piss, and the gods know what else. I remember breathing through my mouth so as not to endure the smell.

"One whiskey, one water, please," Ehrin said, as naturally as possible. I did not think he seemed natural, but he was trying, and the bartender seemed not to notice.

"No whiskey. Just beer," the bartender wheezed between puffs on some rolled tobacco.

"Fine," said Ehrin. "One beer, one water."

The beer was darker than what I had seen my father drink, and I found myself wondering if the brew was dark or if some of the filth of this room had made its way into the glass. My water, however, was clear enough, so I drank. I had not realized how thirsty I was, and I found myself chugging until the glass was empty. The bartender looked at me curiously and then refilled my glass.

He looked at us suspiciously, suddenly, and said, "Listen, I'm going to have to ask you to pay up now. You two look pretty down on your luck. I don't need the two of you drinking and running. Business is down since all this demon business."

"Fine." Ehrin smacked a single coin onto the table. "That should cover a round. It's all I've got. But I have a lute, and I'm good with it."

"No need. Our customers don't want music. They want to be left alone. You won't find many willing to pay for music in Lyncast."

Ehrin, the act dropped for a moment, looked genuinely troubled. "But most people love music. I find it impossible that an entire town could be entirely uninterested."

The bartender, now scrubbing a glass, peered over the top. "In normal times, we might want to have some entertainment. But when a man's stomach is pained with hunger, he cares not for pretty sounds. He wants food. Money buys food, and that means if I'm going to give you beer and water, then I want your money, not your music."

"I won't belabor the point, but it seems to me that the times that try a man's soul are the times when he is in a most dire need of music." I cleared my throat. "Forget it. I understand. How about advice? Can I get that for free?"

The man nodded. "Advice is free, if I have any to give."

"Since Lyncast seems out of the question, do you know of anywhere else around these parts where I can get food and boarding for entertaining the customers? My boy needs to eat. I was thinking of Ferryport, but I never do well in the big cities on account of my face. I was thinking maybe one of the small townships around it. Maybe Poneroy."

"Poneroy? You couldn't make a worse choice than that, my friend. Stay away from there. Madness has descended on that lot. Word came just this morning that they're executing locals on suspicion of consorting with agents of Darkness. A superstitious bunch, if you ask me. A man and his wife were publicly executed, and the townsfolk placed a bounty on the head of a stranger who escaped with their child. And it's getting worse. Two more executions were ordered yesterday. Some are pleading with the authorities in Ferryport to put an end to it, since it's their jurisdiction, but Poneroy has always acted as its own independent hamlet, with its own laws and its own council. I doubt Ferryport will interfere.

"Same person as told me all that said that there's a mood among the people that they don't much like what's happening. There's some whispering about staging a protest, but apparently the two executed yesterday were on the gallows for being too quick to speak in disagreement with the mayor's actions. People didn't much like the family that was killed and drove out, but most realize it could have been any of them accused. But now they're scared to say anything."

He looked at the two of us intently for a moment, and seemed to be considering something. Finally, he said, "No, if I were the two of you, I'd stay away from Poneroy. Go in the opposite direction. Maybe even skip South Hollow. After all, this sort of madness has a tendency to spread like an infection."

So it was that we found ourselves with a hefty bounty on us, and a tavern half-full of people who might have noticed Ehrin's queer appearance and my stunned reaction as the bartender broke to us the story. Ehrin pulled me out hurriedly and we found ourselves once again in flight.

I'll not bother with a lengthy expatiation regarding my grief over the news that my parents had been murdered by those they had called friends, and that I now had no home to return to. It was as ugly and morbid as you might expect, and perhaps more so. But against my most potent of wishes, my life had now forever changed, and there was nowhere to go but forward into the unknown. And I had no one to guide me there but a vagrant musician.

Ehrin did not have the means to take care of a child, but I had nowhere else to go, and Ehrin could never have sent me away. He told me, much later, that he had been haunted by a recurring dream before coming upon my family. In this dream, he had—quite impossibly—been given a son who was to become a gifted musician, and whose music would have a meaningful effect on the world. He never told me details beyond that, except that he was sure from the night of our flight that the dream had been prescient, and that I was that son. Never one to deny the Fates, it was upon him now to determine how he would feed a child when he could barely feed himself.

We found quickly, however, that a child's presence opened purses far more quickly and generously than Ehrin's grimy visage, no matter his ability for music. Besides that, we found that I had quite a gift for dexterity on the strings. He called me a prodigy, although I assumed he was being kind, for my skill came only with great practice—after all, with no other children to call friends, and no other toys than Ehrin's couple of instruments, what else was I to do with my time? Still, I knew I couldn't be bad, because often people would stop in their tracks and stare raptly as I played and sang. Often, when this happened, Ehrin and I both would eat. When I failed, only I would eat, and seeing Ehrin go hungry for my benefit would encourage me to practice that much harder. Before long, he and I were both able to eat fairly regularly, and sometimes we even slept in beds.

We left the Ferryport region behind, and as the grief over my parents relented, somehow, life was good. We had no home, and food was scarce, but we had one another. We were happy.

Little did we know we were still being hunted.

CHAPTER 3

Life was generally peaceful for a time. My musical abilities eventually came to rival Ehrin's, and he was pleased to have a successor who, he thought, had the requisite attractiveness of face and mastery of technique to avoid his own life sentence to poverty. Occasionally, he wrestled with guilt over his inability to provide a stable home, and would suggest that perhaps I should find an appropriate guardian, which I would summarily refuse. I loved my life, and would not have changed a thing. Things, of course, do change, whether we will them to or not. This was a lesson I would soon come to learn once again.

Perhaps if we had lived in another time, we could have held on just a little longer to the life we so enjoyed together. But the emergence of the Fey has touched all of our lives, has it not? I see it in every one of your eyes. It has changed us, and hardened us. Except Ehrin. Ehrin was never hardened. He never changed—except, perhaps, to grow kinder.

***

On my birth date of 14 cycles, Ehrin and I strode confidently into Bordon with stately visages and lofty chins, like a couple of royals bereft of our horses. We were men on a grand adventure, arrived just in time to desecrate the fine city in debaucherous revelry, for I had that very morning reached the age of a man. We had worked extra hard for the past several weeks to put back a little money, and we planned, for this one night of our lives, to spend our earnings as freely as men of means. Ehrin did not often drink, but he did enjoy having fun, and was quite good at it. This was, he informed me, an incredibly special night in a man's life, a night that only comes once, and was worthy of such celebration and merriment.

For those of you who have not had the fortune of visiting Bordon, please allow me to tell you about it, because it is, without a doubt, my favorite city. From miles away, as you crest each hill on the road toward the front gate, you begin to see the telltale patterns of human construction emerge within the distant mountains. A little closer, and you can see giant stone structures jutting from the mountainsides. As you get closer, the ancient stone wall that surrounds the city becomes visible, its crumbling battlements testament to its tremendous age and the immense history of our ancestors' legendary struggles in battle.

Approaching the city gate, you will find three massive stone statues, depicting forgotten heroes of the War of Aradan. One of them depicts the climax of some desperate, long forgotten battle of old. All three of these statues have fallen limbs, lost to slow decay or broken by invading armies over many hundreds of years.

And behind those statues, the city. Bordon is built right into the side of an enormous mountain, stone spires jutting upward and outward, and fortified rooms and passages dug deep within the stone cliffs. Of course, those areas are off-limits to the public and regular citizenry, who occupy the area below, where the ground is flattest and standard structures are built within a giant semicircle extending outward from the base of the mountain.

Bordon was built mostly by the dwarves as a military city, guarding the passageway between East and West, so other than the artistry of those three stone tributes to ancient warriors that stand outside the gates, most of what you see is utilitarian in nature. There is very little that did not once serve some purpose. Many deride it for its lack of aesthetics, but I believe it tells us much about our ancestors. If nothing is built without purpose, then everything built can tell you something about its creators. There is a deep honesty in such practical masonry.

And yet, despite its plainness, its grandness is undeniable. Everything you see is massive in scale, as if built to house a civilization of giants. It is overwhelming, and can make a person feel small.

The most beautiful part of Bordon, however, is its incredible mountainous backdrop, which is the most gorgeous wonder of nature I've encountered. The gray mountains reach far into the sky, dotted and lined with trees that turn a multitude of colors in the fall. Creeks and waterfalls abound, winding their way through canyons and valleys. Natural springs sparkle in the sun and provide crystal clear water like none you have ever tasted. The highest white-capped peaks often stab through the thick, roiling clouds above.

We had chosen Bordon not just for its beauty, or even for its vast expanses of tavern-lined streets, but my birth date just happened to coincide with the local Festival of the Sanctimonious Dwarf. It is the only entirely satirical celebration of a fictional event that I'm aware of, and yet it is among the most raucous occasions I've been a part of. It comes only every seven cycles, so people travel from many leagues around, filling the inns and taverns and spilling out into the streets for a full three days of pure unmitigated decadence. It's sickening…and the most enjoyable experience you will ever have.

Our small savings seemed, to us, a small fortune, and we had determined to have none of that fortune left when the night was through. Breakfast be damned, we would perform hung over for food come morning. And spend our fortune we did. For one brief night, we moved from bar to bar, buying the strongest drink and most delicious of foods. On this night, we were under no pressure to entertain others, but instead indulged for ourselves in the local entertainment. We saw jongleurs, lutists, acrobats, and strongmen. I received my first romantic kiss from a woman of thrice my age, who then pushed my face into such bountiful bosom that at once I felt myself both aroused and wishing to crawl inside her bodice for slumber, upon which she emitted a cackle and smacked my bottom with force enough to propel me back toward the patiently awaiting Ehrin. And from there, the night seems a great blur of grand drama, particularly from the many street performers.

One performance stands out as the brightest memory of the night, and that was a street rendition of The Writhing of the Orlogs, one of the great native dramas of Bordon. I was mesmerized from the very beginning. I had never seen a production so large. At first it seemed a vulgarization of the arts, all spectacle and no substance. But as I soon discovered, that had been a setup. In fact, the play was about an acting troupe performing a well-revered story quite poorly. So when the terrible play-within-a-play ended, the acting and story became engrossing, telling a story of great depth about artists of little talent but great passion. I'll spoil the tale no further, but suffice to say, my mind was pulled in and I could not escape. I do believe, in hindsight, that this was my first experience with magic—whether the actors were aware of it or not. It is often that people are unaware of their own power. When taught the truth of magic, people may realize they've been doing this their entire life, but just hadn't called it magic. When something is done by nature, whether instinctively or because the mind merely happened upon a bit of truth, it is taken for granted. One may even have the false illusion that everyone else sees things the same way. But they're not seeing it, are they?

You're not seeing it yet, are you? Look around you. Pay attention for a moment and think on my words. Is there any part of you that gets what I'm saying, or at least feels the truth of it? You may not fully understand, but even if you just relate, somehow, to what I'm saying, you may be practicing magic. Magic doesn't happen in the thoughts. It happens somewhere deeper, in an unspeakable realm of intuition.

Now, pay close attention. I want you to notice what I've done to your minds. We have all become united. One mind.

I can feel your disbelief. But notice, you can feel the disbelief of the others if you're perceptive. Stop the chattering in your mind and listen closely. It's subtle, because you're all united by the same thoughts and feelings, such that you think it's all your own thoughts. You may be listening to your neighbor's mind and thinking it's your own. It's not. You're all in sync.

So since you're all in sync, listen to me. Listen to my mind.

You still don't quite believe me. Perhaps if you look at my lips, then you'll believe. I stopped talking minutes ago.

But ignore that. Calm.

I want you to just listen. Quiet. Listen.

Quiet your mind. We can all hear you. Don't panic. Just listen to the silence. There. Now you understand.

Those lines came from the most beautiful voice I had ever heard. And despite being words of dialogue from the play, they were also spoken to us, and were no more fiction than the story I tell you now. None of us spoke of it afterwards, but we carried that memory with us.

I learned after the show that her name was Kailee Blehr. She wasn't what most people would call beautiful, but looking at her made me happy. Particularly her smile. It made her beautiful, because every time she smiled, I smiled. I couldn't resist it.

I felt strongly connected to her. I had been pulled into her mind, along with the rest of the audience. And when she mentioned that her lips hadn't been moving, we had all gasped at the truth of this. I know, you're thinking it sounds like an illusion, until you notice that my own lips have stopped moving.

But ignore that. Calm.

I demonstrate only so that you understand how immersed I was in this play, as you are now immersed in my story. You must understand this so that you can understand how badly I wanted to get back into the beautiful mind of Kailee Blehr.

When the show ended, it was like a blow to the gut. One second, I'm falling into this wondrous mind, and the next, I'm shut out. Alone. I felt stranded and lost.

But I didn't have to say anything. She knew. The entire audience knew, because we had all been jolted out of that connected mind. But I did not wander away immediately, because I had felt something the others had not: her interest in me.

Ehrin pulled me away. He knew. He spoke of dangers for the traveling entertainer. There is a rarely spoken rule: don't get attached to anyone who cannot take to the road with you. It leads only to pain. He had suffered such pain once, and hoped that through his own suffering, he could help me to avoid falling into the same fate.

But what, I wondered, if I could get into her troupe? I had never thought about stopping this traveling, but life, I knew, could be much easier. Ehrin would not live forever, and what would I do when he was gone? Would I become old and lonely, as he had been before taking me in? I understood suddenly that I did not have to live as he had. I was a good musician and actor, and a playhouse of that caliber could pay a man quite well. I could settle in this place.

And so, the next morning, I went to the playhouse and asked how to become an actor.

I had a natural skill, and they quickly recognized my potential. They didn't offer me a part initially, but they offered to take me on as an assistant and an apprentice.

Mirkai, the director of the company, owned the theater and was Kailee's father. Given the feelings I had for Kailee, and the curiosity she had shown toward me, this fact made me both nervous and happy. But Mirkai seemed to like me, and calmed my nervousness by telling me that I had more promise than he had seen in someone new to his company, which surprised him, given my lack of formal training. Such training, however, was a necessity even for those privileged with talent, and so lessons were to begin immediately. I was to study under several of the lead actors, including Kailee.

I could tell that Ehrin was crushed when I told him the news, but he kept his composure and congratulated me kindly. I invited him to stay, but he chose to leave. He knew only traveling, and his place was on the road. There was nothing for him here, and I had found a future. He said he would move on in a few days. The goodbye was difficult, but we made empty promises to see one another again soon. And with that, he left.

I was quartered in a small nook under the stairs of the playhouse. It was very small—only enough space for a blanket on the floor—but it was the first place since my parents had died that I could call home. As with so many things in my life, that feeling of home was short-lived. After only a couple of weeks, a letter was slid under my door that changed everything.

CHAPTER 4

I tell my story with the utmost honesty, but I do speak from memory. As such, my narrative is subject to the distortions and biases that plague memory. I can assure you that I remember these events just as I describe them, but if I were to relive one of these moments, I might be surprised to find that the flavor of the event differs in significant ways from how I remember it. I might find that a conversation was worded differently than I've conveyed it this evening. We must all accept that this is simply the nature of storytelling. When done adequately, it is entertaining; when done exceptionally, it is elucidating and even inspiring. But as a perfectly accurate depiction of events, it is flawed.

But I will give you Kailee's words with perfect accuracy, for I still carry her letter, and will simply read it to you. That does not ensure accuracy in her words, but it does ensure accuracy in my portrayal of her letter.

Before I read to you her letter, however, I want you to imagine something for a moment. Imagine that you are born into a theater. You are put on stage from a young age. Your life is devoted, from your earliest of memories, to learning and perfecting convincing characters. You spend a great deal of time under scrutiny by audiences. You must entertain them. You must learn to recite lines with accuracy, and to improvise dramatically when necessary. You must learn to be funny. Most importantly, you must learn to play people's emotions as I play the strings of my lyre.

Now, let's delve a little deeper. You do not have friends outside of the theater. Language, to you, reflects the words of your plays, for you've had limited opportunity to engage in pleasant, casual conversation. You are accustomed to the lofty, dramatic speech of the playwrights, and find that far more natural than the pedestrian prose of the common person.

Think, what would you be like? How would you speak? What would be your conception of love? What sort of story would you make of your own life, and how would you weave in the lives of those who intersect yours?

I will read to you now.

**

Dear Toryn,

Since you came into our theater, my life has been in a state of blissful upheaval. The word upheaval is treated poorly, is it not, with its typically negative connotations? As a young woman utterly lacking in adventure, I find it lovely.

But this I know: The loveliness will fade, and gloom will settle back over my home if I do not leave this dreadful place before this moment of upheaval is gone. I must go, Toryn, and soon.

I've visited many places and experienced many wonderful and terrifying things vicariously through the troupe's fantastical plays. And yet, I've never left the immediate vicinity of this theater.

You've inspired me, Toryn, and offered me hope. I've told you so little of what I've endured in this prison of a theater. I've suffered great misery at the hands of my father, and now I plan to leave, just as you've set your will on staying. This cannot be. I cannot let your spirit be dulled, as it surely will if you stay. Please, come with me. Let us escape together.

Before we met, I had long given up hope of ever seeing lands beyond Bordon, or even beyond this small city block. I have never been that far, and that is because my father will never allow it. For most of my years, I took for granted that this was simply the natural way of things. In order to live, one need learn the craft of one's parents and carry on that tradition from generation to generation, without ever leaving one's roots behind.

But you. You and Ehrin. You were so free—far freer than the miserable travelers for whom I regularly perform. You sang, and you told stories, just as I do, but you carried your art with you. You were tethered to nothing, as I wish to be. I'm positive that if you were cast into a hellish netherworld of pure cruelty and pain, you would still find peace in your craft, so blessed are you with freedom.

And yet, as I behold such beauty that my eyes threaten to spill their wetness down my cheeks at the mere thought of the blessings you've been granted, you curse and cast off this gift, preferring to stay here to serve my malevolent father. And why? Because you've spent these many years wishing for a home? What is it you want from this place, Toryn? Fame? Stability? The love of my family? To be accepted as one of us? Perhaps you will find fame here, but you will never find love.

Yet, despite such infinite odds of finding what you truly seek, you've given up what to achieve these ends? More than is imaginable to me. I've watched you sacrifice a beautiful man who gave you love of a depth I've not before encountered. A man who was the family you seek, and who chose that role despite owing you nothing. A more wonderful soul I have not met, and you allowed him to march from the gates with lute and sack, off into the open world, while you remained here—just so that you might sleep in a bed. I find myself struggling with a depth of feeling for you, Toryn, and yet for this, I hate you. That for which I would have given up everything, you cast off in exchange for a fleeting comfort.

In but two nights, I'll be leaving my home of ten and seven cycles, and I know not where I go, nor do I care. I'll do my best to find the direction in which Ehrin departed, and if I find him, I'll see if I might join him in his travels. If I don't find him, then I'll travel on my own, and I'll perform in exchange for trifles. And I'll appreciate the great freedom I have gained in life, because I'll have known well its dreadful alternative.

I leave on this journey with or without you, Toryn, but I'm hoping that you will join me. Please, don't be lured in by the false hopes of this cadaverous opera house. Just because you have not yet developed the sense to smell it does not mean it does not wreak of the death of a thousand dreams. I live with it every day, and every moment of it is nauseating.

If you choose to come, then I have a plan. You may not care for my plan, as it involves taking something dear to my father. When you see this thing, however, you will agree that taking it is the right thing to do. Believe me, Toryn, when I say that my father is not who you think he is, and if you let me, I will prove it to you, then free us from his reach.

Meet me in the side alley two nights from now when the red moon is at its highest, and I'll explain. If you don't show up, I'll assume that you have chosen your pillow over freedom, and will accept your decision. If you do show up, then our lives will surely become interesting.

CHAPTER 5

I chose to stay. And I chose not to see this mysterious relic that Kailee had decided to steal. I chose not to see Kailee at all. I had made my decision, and I would not leave theater life behind without first giving it a chance. Besides that, I was learning from the best in the craft.

The following day—the day before Kailee's planned theft and departure—I discovered that her letter had gone missing. Upon coming back from breakfast, my tiny room had been cleaned by one of the maids, and the letter had been taken. I certainly did not intend to betray Kailee, but I do sometimes believe that the depths of my mind had conspired to sabotage her escape, so that we could all remain in my new home that I so loved. How easily I could have hidden the note, or even burned it. Instead, I had left it open upon my small trunk of clothes. Of course it was discovered, and of course it would be read. And once read, of course it would be delivered to Mirkai. My heart shattered with the realization of my betrayal.

I careened down the hallway to Kailee's room, but her door was open and she was not inside. I raced to the dressing rooms, the practice hall, the main stage, and the cafeteria, but she was nowhere to be found.

I bolted downstairs to the cellar, where I found her sitting next to a trapdoor in the floor. A rug had been thrown to the side, clearly meant to hide the entrance to whatever was below.

"Toryn! You came." She seemed not only happy, but relieved.

"Kailee, your letter. I'm sorry. Somebody found it. I left it lying out without thought."

"It's okay," she assured me. "I saw the maid carrying it and took it from her." She handed it to me, and I quickly placed it in my pocket. "This just means we have to go now. I was sitting here trying to figure out some way to get your attention without arousing suspicion, and now, here you are." Her face was lit up with that beautiful smile, and I found myself wanting nothing more than to run with her, despite not understanding what we were running from. It could mean a life with her, and that was all that mattered at that moment.

She pointed to the trapdoor. "I've gotten the door unlocked. As soon as I get what I need, we'll be free. If we're caught afterwards, I can handle it. I promise."

She pulled up on the trapdoor with an attached chain, lifting it, then tipping it over with her other hand until it stood upright, held back from falling in the other direction by another chain underneath. She began to descend a steep set of stairs into the pitch darkness below. I took one step behind her, and then froze. I couldn't do it. My guilt overwhelmed me. I was not a thief who stole from a man who took me in then fled into the night with the man's daughter.

She saw the struggle on my face. "Toryn, please. You mustn't waste time. If you trust me, then please, help me, and I'll explain once we're well away from this place. I promise, you'll not only understand my desperation, but you'll be glad you got away with me."

"I'm sorry, Kailee," I said. "No. I can't let you steal from your father, who has been so kind to me. Perhaps you have some explanation, and I trust that you do, because I trust you. But Ehrin, who you spoke so highly of in your letter, raised me better than to take from a man who has done me no harm. Perhaps you may convince me that he has ill intentions for me. But then I must consider that perhaps, even if you're right, he will change his mind. That is a chance I must give him. And even if he fails me, then I'll simply leave. I won't take that which does not belong to me. I've done many things to survive on the streets, but I've never resorted to thievery."

She considered, and then nodded sadly. "Fine. Then just pretend you didn't see me. When you've learned your lesson, you can come find me."

"Kailee, I don't think you're listening to me. By telling me your plan, you've made me complicit in your crime. I cannot possibly walk away and do nothing, and I will not lie."

"Oh, Toryn, you don't understand."

"Then you have until we're discovered to help me understand."

I took a seat and reclined, as if settling in patiently for a long show. She sighed. "Fine." She climbed back up a few steps and sat on the floor, with her feet resting two steps below. "I'll tell you the story. I understand this ethical quandary of yours, however absurd I might find it, and I won't expect you to aid me in my theft. But I hope that after hearing my story, you'll just pretend you haven't seen me and let me slip away. Honesty is noble, but when you condemn a person to suffer so that you might continue feeling good and superior for that lofty nobility, then your ethics are questionable."

CHAPTER 6

My father was always obsessed with fame and fortune. He was born into an acting family, as was I, and he was quite good.

He discovered, or so he believed, that those who are best at acting are either severe psychopaths, or they are extreme empaths. Psychopaths are good at pretending, while empaths are good at reading an audience, detecting subtle cues, and so on—as long as they can manage to suspend their self-consciousness and immerse themselves in the role.

The theater has been in my family for several generations, and has been a staple of Bordon for at least two centuries. Under my father, its success fluctuated greatly as he learned how to run it as a business. At some point, however, it no longer mattered how well he ran it...the people had simply begun to lose interest in theater. I believe it was around the same time as those creatures emerged from the abyss, and anxieties were high. One would think that people would want nothing more than to escape into our fictional worlds, but instead they chose to stay home. I believe our fantastical stories became, rather than an escape, a reminder of the troubling reality that was springing into the world from our collective nightmares. Whatever the cause, business began to dry up, and for the first time in its history, the theater was facing closure.

One day, a man arrived who introduced himself as "the collector." I assume that my father eventually learned the man's real name, but I still know him only as the collector. The man proclaimed himself a devoted patron of the arts, and brought to my father a gift: a crimson colored mask that he claimed held great power. The man wanted to save the arts in Bordon, and claimed that this mask could make the theater famous once again. Perhaps, even, the most well known theater in history.

My father was skeptical, but intrigued, and ultimately his curiosity got the better of him. He paid the man a small deposit to keep the mask on loan until he could try it out, with the rest to be paid after its powers were confirmed. The collector did not hesitate to accept this offer, so confident was he.

The following weekend, my father wore the mask during his performance. People seemed enthralled by the mask, as it was quite beautiful and radiated some strange aura of attraction. Beyond that, however, it seemed nothing happened. The people cheered, but only in their usual semi-attentive way.

My father went to the collector and demanded his money back, but was persuaded to try one more test. "Try letting your wife wear the mask," he said. So at the next week's show, he did just that. At first, my mother was uncomfortable to be wearing a mask at all, as she was quite vein and believed her beautiful visage should be front and center. The audience sensed her discomfiture and became restless. So she locked eyes with one person in the crowd, and began to sing to him. His body relaxed into his seat, and his eyes focused on hers intently. Only when she had him fully attentive did she move her gaze to the next person, and then the next, one after the other until the entire audience appeared spellbound.

At the end of the performance, the audience erupted into a chorus of cheers, the fervor of which this theater had never seen. After the show, the locals in attendance approached the staff and demanded to be first in line to the next week's show, and so advance tickets were sold, and the show was quickly sold out.

The next day, my father paid the collector the rest of his due and kept the mask.

From that point, word of mouth spread across the lands. The theater grew in popularity, and eventually they had to begin doing monthly performances outdoors in vast open spaces like the one you first saw me in, just to accommodate everyone traveling from afar. Just a few years later, Blehr Theater had become the most famous theater in all of the lands—just as the collector had promised.

My mother soon discovered that she no longer needed the mask. Over time, she had internalized the ability. This gave my father an idea: if everyone in the cast had my mother's abilities, then there would be no limits to the fame the company could achieve. So he tried having others wear the mask. Interestingly, it worked for none of them. My parents wondered if, perhaps, it would only work for people with some particular trait or aptitude. Perhaps my mother was doing something that the others weren't, though try as they might, they could not find anything different.

So every night, without explaining why, a different person in the troupe would be asked to wear the mask. When they ran out of resident cast members, they began doing one-night-only stand-ins for talent around the area, under the pretense of consideration for expanding the residency. Every person who tried it failed. My parents began to wonder if the mask had been powerless all along, and perhaps it had merely unlocked some latent powers that my mother had already possessed.

The collector, visiting one evening, made a passing remark that stunned my father, for he had not considered it. "Perhaps," the collector said, "it's in the blood. You should let your daughter try the mask." I had just reached an age at which some mild ambition had formed, and I had been pleading with my parents to let me join the performances. Now, they agreed. First, they began giving me occasional roles, whenever a scene called for a small girl, or when they could wedge one into a storyline. They discovered, of course, that I was a natural talent and that I had a way with the crowd.

After only a dozen or so performances, they had me wear the mask, and I stole the show.

I remember that night with such clarity. The audience was enthralled, and at the age of seven, I worked that crowd like a true master.

Only one performance later, I stripped off the uncomfortable mask and looked around at the eyes of the crowd to find them all staring back, eyes wide with wonder, as if lost in the depths and mysteries of my world. And it was true. They were lost, and had given themselves to me fully, trusting me to guide them to whatever fictional reality I wished. That is a sort of trust and intimacy that seems inappropriate for a crowd to give some stranger on a stage, and yet, there it was. Had I been a malicious person, I could have caused them great suffering. Perhaps madness, such was their abdication of control to me. But instead, I took them to pleasant places, and they thanked me wordlessly. This I accomplished, now, without the mask. I did not need it.

The irony, as I look back upon that night—and every performance since—is that the particular sort of magic I exerted on them made them love me. Had it been any other sort of magic, they would have seen me burn. One might argue that my magic is less visible, and therefore it is ignorance that saves me from them, but we both know better, don't we? You've seen it yourself. They know, and they don't care, or they don't admit it, because I've taken away their fear. They trust me. And so they look the other way at my magic, and even come back for more, while executing others. Sometimes on the same evening. People see what they want to see.

As I grew older, I wanted to use my talent for something greater than mere entertainment. More importantly, I wanted to experience the world beyond these walls, and beyond this city. But my mother's age was beginning to show, and my father needed a young star to work the crowd into the proper sort of frenzy. As my body began to develop, especially, he began to put me into seductive roles, and I hated every moment. It fed my desire to leave, but when once I tried, I discovered that my feelings of imprisonment here were, in fact, the reality.

It turns out that my father's relationship with the collector had continued well beyond the acquisition of that mask. We sit now, Toryn, atop a network of catacombs that reach deep into the ground in a vast reticulum of interconnecting stairways and tunnels. Nobody seems to know, including my father, when or why they were built, but they are certainly quite ancient.

This theater has been in my family for many generations, and when my ancestor, Jed Blehr, first made the purchase, it had been the home of a reclusive man of questionable mental faculties. Upon that man's death, Jed purchased the land, and this building was erected. Even during construction, the catacombs were not discovered, despite the cellar being dug a mere eleven feet above the massive underground chamber below us. That chamber is important, because from there, all paths lead down, further into the ground, such that this is the location with the shortest path into the catacombs. But no one knew this.

Except the collector. Somehow, he knew. "Dig into the earth beneath the cellar," he told my father, "and you will find a room. From this room, you will find a labyrinthine, twisting mass of tunnels, which could not be explored in your lifetime. Within these tunnels, you will find the remains of an ancient civilization. And in these remains, you will find artifacts of great, long-lost power."

This information came at a cost, however. The collector was but one member, it turned out, of a secretive sect of the Forsworn, who are bent on collecting such artifacts of power and using them to some end that even my father does not seem to fully know.

My father was inducted into their organization, and they told him that he would be Chair of the Bordon Chapter of the Forsworn—a position I believe fabricated to give him a false sense of importance, when really his only job is to guard and maintain the catacombs below and keep the theater running as a facade. That had been their aim from the start. Men shrouded in wide-brimmed hats and layered capes come and go in secret through an underground passage I discovered while following my father. They disappear into this very hole, and sometimes do not emerge for hours or even days. I believe that now it is mostly used as a storage facility and occasional meeting place. Many artifacts are discovered down there, and there's no need to take them anywhere else. Meanwhile, many more are brought in from other places.

I believe they also consider the depths below to be ideal for experimenting with these items, as I do not believe they are very knowledgeable about their uses. In my eavesdropping, I've heard a great deal of speculation. They may be as ignorant about the mechanics of these artifacts as you and me.

My father once caught me spying, and soon after, he caught me trying to escape. He warned me that I'd better keep quiet, and not ever try to leave, because the men in the Sworn were dangerous. They were not only counting on access to the catacombs below, but also on our ability to attract great numbers of people—for reasons he never disclosed. But they clearly have something planned, and I don't believe the outcome will be pleasant. We're planting seeds in our many patrons' minds, to some end that I'm unaware, but I am sure I would not care for it if I knew. Since my mother has aged, and I'm the only person left able to channel the power of the mask, they need me. Whatever they're doing, they can't do it without me. And yet I want no part in it.

My father told me that without the mask nearby, my abilities would quickly fade. I would find myself with no skills to support myself, and I would starve. And if the Sworn ever found me, they would bring me back, and they might torture me to make sure I never try to leave again.

When you came, Toryn, I quickly saw a way out of all of it. You and Ehrin, I found, possessed a raw and natural talent, but it was not bestowed by some artifact. I knew that, even without the mask's power, I could still make my way by virtue of my passion and natural abilities—as you and Ehrin have. I know it is not a glamorous life, but I don't mind that. I just want to be free.

Still, I would not bring harm to you, or to myself. Besides that, I have to try to thwart whatever plan my father and the Sworn have set to, since they are manipulating thousands of innocent people. To know it's happening and yet do nothing is to be complicit in their crime, is it not? You used this very argument just moment ago. Well, which is the greater crime?

The mask is the answer. Without its power, and without my power, their plan fails. And with the mask, my abilities would be amplified. I could easily convince any agent of the Sworn to look the other way as I escape. In fact, if I chose to, I could make that person fall so deeply in love with me that he or she would never be likely to betray me, even under great duress.

If it assuages your conscience, just know that the mask does not belong to my father to begin with. It belonged to an ancient people. The collector acquired it, but that does not mean it was his to sell. I'm told that there is an association of historians among the Druidic Council that protects and studies these sorts of things—openly, and without nefarious aims. If I am able to find them, after I'm safe, then I will give the mask to them.

Toryn, please, the telling of this tale has taken far too long. You have to make a decision, and I hope it's the right one. Help me find the mask, and let's flee this place before we're discovered. I have two sets of paupers' clothes and wigs in my bag, and we can be out of the city gates before my father raises an alarm.

CHAPTER 7

"So what is your plan?" I asked her.

She smiled with relief and joy. "Simple. We get the mask, and we walk out of here quietly. Once we're out of the city, we run. We find Ehrin. We travel around, entertaining people as we go. We avoid the Sworn. And if we run into trouble, I politely suggest they let us be."

"Okay, that works for me. Let's go, then."

I followed her down the stairs and into the unknown below. The still, musty air stank dully of dirt, mold, and mildew. Through the otherwise perfect silence, I could hear water dripping in the distance, its single repeating note echoing down a dozen corridors. The darkness was suffocating until, upon reaching a level floor, she lit an oil lantern that was ensconced in a cleft in the wall. Its orange flame sputtered for a few moments, then steadied.

I was astonished to find myself in a room whose opposite wall was only dimly reached by the light of the torch, so spacious was it. In the center of the room was an enormous oak table that seemed quite impossible, as there was no entrance large enough through which to carry it in. Around the table were a number of chairs, and on the table was a scattering of papers.

Along the wall was a series of shelves carved into the stone, upon which sat various items of obvious antiquity. Between many of those shelves hung enormous tapestries of rich violet with elaborate patterns of intricate detail. No normal theater, it occurred to me, could afford so much purple fabric or dye, and if it could, it would certainly not hang the tapestries in this humid, secret room beneath its cellar.

Kailee pulled the lantern from its lodging and began walking the circumference of the room to our right, passing shelf after carved shelf of odd paraphernalia. On the first shelf sat a silvery chalice, ancient and unpolished, with barbs protruding around its lip that would make it impossible to drink from without stabbing oneself. Next was a simple, beaded necklace around the neck of a velvety bust display—a fine stand, it seemed, for such a simple item. Next was a shiny serrated arrowhead of what appeared to be a naturally mauve-colored stone, sitting alone on its oversized shelf. Next was a smoothly carven short wooden rod with a ferrule of a metal like bluish silver, carved with swirling patterns that reminded Toryn of smoke in a light breeze.

Then we passed the first tunnel, which extended into the unknown darkness. I was tempted to explore, but Kailee grabbed my sleeve and pulled me forward. "He keeps it in here. If we explore, we'll get lost." I nodded and followed her.

We came next to a shelf containing a glass eye. As I glanced at it, I could swear it was looking back at me. Of course, a glass eye with a lacquered iris pointed in my direction is probably going to cause that illusion, but as I moved, it seemed to follow me. I took a step backward, and then a step forward, and no matter what angle I was at, it still seemed to be looking in my direction, though it did not seem to move.

We hurried away from that shelf to the next, which contained an unadorned and uncarved branch from a tree—strangely dull after everything else we had seen. I reached out to touch it, and she smacked my hand. "I wouldn't." I didn't ask, but simply followed her past it.

Next was a golden box etched with detailed latticework, which Kailee stopped to open, but found empty. This, she began to pocket, but I reminded her that we were not petty thieves and would leave with only with the singular item that we agreed to take with us. She nodded and continued.

Several more shelves contained more assorted items that I've since forgotten, and along the way we passed another hallway extending into darkness.

Finally, at a third of the way around the circumference of the chamber, we came to a shelf that contained a beautiful mask of crimson-lacquered wood, with intricate patterns inlaid in an opalescent red metal that I had never seen. Somehow, as I moved around the shelf, its expression first appeared loving and kind from one angle, then angry and fierce from another. It was perhaps the most beautiful item I have ever gazed upon.

As Kailee stood staring at the mask, I began to grow nervous. We had, I realized, stayed for far too long. It struck me for the first time that, if her stories were even partially true, we were in grave danger if we were caught. I said her name, but she continued to stare silently, in deep reverie, as if in a trance. She wanted, it appeared, to savor this moment, but for that, there was no time. I touched her arm lightly, and she lifted the mask and began to put it onto her face.

Something told me this was not the right moment, and that she was succumbing to some unworldly temptation. So I grabbed the mask from her hands, startling her from her trance, and told her to follow me.

I ran up the stairs without another word, and could hear her footsteps close behind me. As I emerged through the trapdoor, however, a foot struck me across my face, sending me sprawling to the floor, and the trapdoor was slammed shut behind me. I looked up through moistened eyes to find Mirkai looming over me. He kept his foot on the trapdoor as he bent down and bolted it shut. It rattled as Kailee struggled against it from below, but understanding that it was a waste of time, she quickly gave up. We were caught.

"Don't move." He was alone, but he had a rapier leveled at me. I'm no fighter, so I knew better than to move. Without taking his eyes from me, he backed up a couple of steps and grabbed a chair, sliding it across the stone floor until it was on top of the trapdoor, and sat in it.

"Grab that other chair and sit," he told me. "You need to know, I've been listening all along. I've been wondering for some time what sort of plan that girl was hatching, but I find myself surprised at the extent of her deceit. So the first thing I'm going to do is correct a couple of her more egregious lies. Then you're going to walk out of here and take that mask—but not my daughter—with you."

"Sir," I began, but a twitch of the blade was warning to cease speaking. I pulled the other chair in front of him and sat quietly.

"Now I need you to listen closely to me, boy. If, at the end of this talk, I feel like you've understood me, I'm going to let you walk out of here with that mask. If I don't feel like you've understood me, I'm going to slice that throat of yours, and your body will go into those caverns below, to never be seen again. Anyone asks, I'll just tell them you went looking for that mentor of yours, just like you planned on doing. Maybe demons ate you out on those roads at night. No one would be suspicious. Lots of murders being blamed on those creatures these days. Am I clear?"

I nodded.

A distant voice came to me—it was Kailee, calling from beneath the trapdoor. I felt myself pulled to her, but the blade reminded me not to move.

"I know you want to go to her, and that feeling will get stronger. I know what my daughter can do. So you're going to resist it long enough for me to talk. If you submit to her and go for this door, you die. So hold yourself real tight to that chair for a little while. Do you understand?"

Again, I nodded.

"It's true," he began, "that I've not been a good man or a good father. My youthful obsession with fame and fortune has led me to this, and for that, I'm burdened by a thousand regrets…"

CHAPTER 8

My wife and I were much too young when my father passed away and left me this theater. It happened quite suddenly. Gracen and I were but children experiencing our first taste of love, free from obligation or concern, and suddenly thrust into responsibility for the well-being and success of our troupe. It was a trying time, and we had many failures.

Gracen's mother, Darha, was an actress here before Gracen was born—and a fine one, at that. She was a stunning beauty, and attracted many patrons with her sultry and seductive acts. I do not remember her well, but I'm told she had a deep and powerful but feminine voice with a rasp that people found irresistible. When she spoke, men were allured and women were either inspired or envious. When she sang, emotions would boil over. All in all, she was great for business.

Darha knew, however, that she would not remain a beauty forever. So when wealthy or powerful men passed through, she would flirt. This means, of course, that she bedded many wealthy and powerful men. None ever took her as a wife, however. Instead, she became pregnant, and could only guess at who the father might be. This is a minor scandal for an actress, as we're expected some degree of prurience, but it did take her off the market for marriage into affluence.

I vaguely remember the uproar around the theater, as I was three cycles at the time. A pregnant main attraction is far less enticing to many of the patrons, so my father was agitated around that period. Still, our troupe is our family, and we support one another, both materially and emotionally, so she was well cared for during her pregnancy.

When Gracen was born, her mother bled, and the physician could not stop the bleeding. She died in the dressing room, where they had setup a makeshift delivery area. I remember hearing the cries, and seeing the body, wrapped in a long white sheet, crimson-soaked in its center, carried out. I snuck quietly to the door, peaked inside, and saw the simpering baby being rocked by one of the stagehands in a chair in the far corner of the room while another stagehand poured buckets of water on the floor, rinsing the blood down the shower drain. From that point, and for some time, the theater became a somber place.

My father called everyone together the following morning and announced that Gracen would be a child of the theater. The troupe would be her collective parents. And so it was. Everyone loved Gracen, and everyone took turns caring for her, teaching her, playing with her, and generally spoiling the girl. In short, I was jealous. Before Gracen came along, I had been the baby, and now they had a new baby.

Once she was weaned and no longer needed the constant attention of a nanny, I often had to babysit her, as everyone in the troupe was busy with practice and shows. When she was two, I was only five, but I considered myself quite responsible. I could feed her, change her when she had accidents, teach her to count, and read to her, and I did these things without complaint. When she was around three, I started teaching her to act by having her try out different emotions on various people. This invariably worked. If she panicked at the sight of an invisible mouse, the actors also panicked. If she cried appropriately, she could garner the most operatic of sympathy from the dramatically inclined troupers. Soon, I had her mimicking all of the emotions that can be described.

As we grew, she became my best friend. We spent almost all of our time together, and we were good to one another. Most in the troupe thought of her as my sister, and perhaps she was something of a sister. But she was also a friend. Eventually, she became something more.

We were both actors, of course. Her roles were still small at this time, and I had mastered all of my parts, so neither of us bothered much with rehearsal. That left most of our days free to enjoy one another's company. And our favorite pastime was to hike through the mountains outside of the city.

There are many trails through the mountains. Some of them are meant for going places, and others are there merely for Bordoners to walk and see the sights. Gracen and I preferred leaving the trails behind. We enjoyed the idea that perhaps we were going places where no human being had ever set foot. It didn't hurt that we were afforded great privacy, which is how Kailee was later conceived. But not just yet.

At the age of seventeen cycles, my father passed away of heart failure. I had never had a mother—my father never spoke of her, but I believe she left him when I was just a baby—so I found myself without parents. The theater, now, was mine to run. I did not want the responsibility, and was not ready for it. And we almost lost it for my negligence.

Gracen and I began to throw parties after hours. We would fill the hall with people we enjoyed, and afterwards, we would often retire with a handful of people to our chambers—the massive bedroom that had recently belonged to my father.

The staff was patient with us, as we had grown up among them, and they loved us as family. But stress ran high. We were bleeding money, as I had no clue how to run such a business. We spent far too much on our parties, and if not for the experienced staff, the entire operation would have collapsed around us. What I have now, I owe entirely to them.

This went on for several years, and I did become better. I felt an obligation not to let them down, and so I tried. I began accepting advice from some of the older members of the troupe, enlisted a great deal of help with the finances, and began to scale back the nighttime festivities.

Gracen and I continued to hike, when we could. When I was twenty-two cycles, and Gracen just recently nineteen, as we were hiking through some particularly remote terrain that we had never been through, we came across a fellow hiker, sitting upon a small shelf in the rock midway up the leeward side of a moss-smothered butte. He wore a collection of shabby rags for clothes, though his boots were thick and sturdy. He sat by the remains of a campfire and was very still, gazing in the direction of Bordon, though the sight was blocked by a larger mountain.

We were upon him before he noticed our presence. Still, when I coughed lightly to alert him, he seemed unsurprised and did not alter his gaze before speaking calmly.

"Have a seat," he said. We sat nearby, me to his left, and Gracen to mine, with our feet dangling from the edge of the shelf. "Your people amaze me," he said with a forlorn shake of his head. "They live in the midst of such beauty in these rocky and forested peaks and valleys, and yet most of them remain willfully bound by the confines of that city and that dreadful perimeter wall. Such contentment with banality and endless repetition of well-rehearsed daily routines, when they're but a few short steps from the freedom of these mountain passes. But not you two. You are exceptions. Here you are, venturing into the unknown, away from the safety, security, and boredom of the city."

At the moment, I found myself confused by his speech and wasn't sure how to respond. I told him as much, but thanked him for allowing us a break from our climb. I hoped that would end this line of conversation and we could enjoy our view.

"I think you do understand me," he continued. "Otherwise, you would be sitting in some restaurant down there, downing mugs of ale in order to forget for a moment how dull and repetitive your lives have become. Instead, you're here, gazing with a stranger upon the magnificence of nature that your brethren below have long forgotten."

"Yes," I heard Gracen say with a wavering voice. "I feel like a prisoner in that city, knowing that even if I left, I'd find myself in the same prison in another city. I long for freedom. That is why I remain an actor. The fictions give me a brief escape. So fleeting is that relief. But this…"

"This requires no effort of imagination," he answered. "This simply exists, and as we sit, we can let our minds stop their chatter for a moment, and just observe."

With that, our chatter stopped, and we sat quietly for some time.

"It is good that you found me," he eventually resumed, "for otherwise I would have been forced into that odious place you call a city to find you."

"You must have us mixed up, my friend," I informed him. "I'm sorry, but we do not know you."

"You are Mirkai, of the house Blehr, owner of Blehr

Theater. Son of the famous Borgham. And you are Gracen, resident cast member of Blehr Theater. I know you, and so do my employers, who told me that I might find you out here. My name is Saret Starn, and I am a messenger."

We demanded to know the identity of his employer, but he refused. Instead, his tone turned serious, and he began to speak the words of an insane person.

"It matters not who buys my food. It matters only that you heed my words. A symphony of interconnecting events is now underway, all of which have been orchestrated by a brilliant mind, the owner of which you may someday meet.

"I'm afraid your days of frolicking in the mountains is over. Please believe me when I say that I grieve for your loss, man of nature that I am. I wish you a life of freedom, and for this reason, I very much resent my employer for this task. It will be my last for the organization. And yet, if I do not deliver this last message, then I put you both in danger along with myself.

"Enjoy this last vacation from the city. I'll leave you my camp and enough supplies to stay for a couple of days. Savor it, for when you return to the city, you will never leave those walls again. If you attempt to leave, the organization that hired me will see you dead and your family's theater will become theirs. Such is within their power.

"Most importantly, that child that is now in your belly, Gracen, must never be allowed to leave the immediate vicinity of that theater. She must be protected, and she must be contained. If you fail at this, then my employers will see to it, and my guess is that this would become unpleasant."

Although we thought him a lunatic spouting nonsense, he turned out to be correct about Gracen's pregnancy. She was one month pregnant with Kailee, to be exact. This insane man, rambling nonsense, had known…and I still cannot say how. Even at that moment, despite our disbelief, his tone had shaken us. He seemed so sure, so lucid, and he knew us. We remained silent, unsure of how to proceed. He did not seem dangerous, but his words certainly were.

He looked at the ground, looking regretful. "Please believe me when I say that this is not my will. Were it up to me, I would destroy the organization that hired me and set the two of you free. But that is not within my power.

"But please also believe me when I tell you that my words are truth. This organization is powerful, their agents are in every city watching their interests, they are ruthless in the execution of their goals, and they have come to the decision that you must do as I've asked. If you don't, you'll suffer grave consequences."

Still, we stood quietly. Gracen grabbed my hand and squeezed, her mouth working as if trying to think of some appropriate way to respond, but finding none.

"I will leave you here," he said, "and you will not see me again. For that matter, neither will my employers, now that my final task for them is complete. I will travel far beyond their reach and attempt to find a life of peace.

"But you will be visited again, by a man I know only as the collector. I've met him, and he is not a bad man, considering the company he keeps among his organization. I would recommend that you trust him, and do as he asks. He has told me that he will come with a gift, but not until the correct time. Accept it, and do what he says."

He looked reflective for a moment, and then brightened, only slightly. "You may choose to look at this as an opportunity. Upon entering into an agreement with my employers, you will be thereafter protected. Your every need will be met. You will achieve fame and fortune. You will have status in both the organization and the city of Bordon. So, too, will your daughter have these things. You will be a tool in the schemes of the organization, but other than these few instructions, you will be free to continue life as you have, minus your excursions beyond the city walls. All in all, this is not the worst fate a couple such as yourselves could suffer. Many may even envy you for this."

Without another word, the man walked back the way Gracen and I had come and disappeared around a bend. True to his word, we never saw him again.

When we returned to the theater, two days later, we agreed that we would ignore the man's instructions. He was, after all, merely an insane man we met in the mountains, wearing rags for clothing. Only equally insane people would trust such a man. And yet, the responsibilities of the theater became such that we never got around to going on another hike.

After eight months, Kailee was born, and Gracen and I once again felt love in our hearts. We also experienced fear, although we never spoke of it, for we both knew that the birth lent some credence to the mysterious man's words.

Of course, the collector did appear. An interesting character, this man. He looked strangely familiar to us, but we would surely have remembered such a man. Perhaps, we considered, we had seen him before amongst the audience. He was tall and gaunt, made even taller by a shiny black top hat. An eye patch covered his right eye; his left eye was bright blue and appeared most discerning. Carefully trimmed facial hair ran from the sides of his face, down his cheeks, then up to his upper lip, leaving his lower jaw bare — a gentleman's shave, which I have since tried to emulate, quite unsuccessfully.

As promised, he delivered to us a gift: that mask you now hold in your hands. He told us that it was for our daughter, but we refused it. He said that the mask had great power, and we said that was all the more reason to refuse, as it could prove a dangerous item. He nodded his understanding, and recommended that we try it for ourselves to prove that it was not dangerous, and with reluctance, we agreed.

For me, the mask did nothing; for Gracen, it seemed to give an uncanny connection with the minds of those around her. Its value to a performer was undeniable, and we did, as Kailee told you, lust for fame. So we accepted the gift, and as foretold, found ourselves locked into a binding agreement with the shadowy organization, which we now knew was called the Forsworn. Forsworn to what, I have only clues, but this is what they call themselves. You have probably heard of them, or at least seen their symbol — a five pointed star with a hammer and sword. This symbol adorns their temples in every major city, although they go mostly ignored.

Membership is open to anyone, but climbing the ranks of the organization requires vows of secrecy and lifelong loyalty. One must be in the leadership to find out what their true aims are. Suffice to say, I am not in their upper ranks.

The collector decided that we should take our time in introducing the mask to Kailee. Gracen, he said, should wear it for a period. Only after we were entirely comfortable with it should we give it to Kailee. But do not, he warned, wait too long.

At this point, we had become concerned over Kailee's increasingly manipulative nature. She and Gracen both had that uncanny ability to move people, but they accomplished this for very differing reasons, and to very differing ends. Gracen, I had long known, had a way with people because she was so in tune with them. She, more than any person I've known—and I've known many people—has a way of seeing the world from other people's perspectives, and feeling what they're feeling. It was what attracted me to her. She is incredibly empathic, and people can sense that. They open up to her, and they trust her without giving it much thought, for they can sense that she would never abuse that trust. She makes them feel safe. The mask seemed to amplify that ability. She used the mask for a few shows, but began to feel guilty for the power the mask gave her, and was disturbed by the temptations it spawned, so she placed it in a drawer and swore never to wear it again. But its effect lingered. I'm not sure it has worn off entirely to this day.

Kailee, we had found, seemed to have the exact same way with people that Gracen did. She knew exactly what to say to people to make them feel better, or to establish a rapport with them. We were pleased with this, for a time, until we began to suspect that it was mere pretense. She did not get into people's minds with the caring empathy of her mother, but through pure acting. She did not feel what she seemed to feel, but was able to perfectly emulate the outward appearance of feelings. She had watched and studied people and their interactions. She learned to dissect what people's body language, expressions, and words really meant to them, and discovered how to react in ways to get what she wanted from them. She was a masterful manipulator, and a natural strategist. She had, we felt, no regard for the well being of others, except to the extent that those people's well being suited her purposes.

For all of her abilities, however, my wife was still better, and Kailee's jealousy festered. We had told her of the mask, and hinted at its properties. Before thinking better of it, we had told her that, once the appropriate time came, the mask would become hers.

One night, before a show, she asked us to let her wear it, but of course, we refused. Several weeks later, as we were performing The Gift of the De'eru one evening, Gracen and I were well into the third act when Kailee strode brazenly onto the stage wearing the mask. Not only had she stolen it from Gracen's drawer, and then confronted us in public with her betrayal, but we were helpless to say or do anything about it, as hundreds of eyes were upon us. She had done this with calculated intent, and her eyes revealed her satisfaction through the slits in the mask. The veil of innocence had dropped, and before us stood our daughter in her true form.

We may have been willing to ruin the play for that one night, but we could not risk revealing the mask. So we had no choice but to continue the scene, and to improvise. We welcomed her into the scene, and she proceeded to take over. There was a battle for the minds of the audience between my wife and my masked daughter, and I could only watch in horror as my daughter stole the show. By the end of the scene, all eyes were locked on Kailee, and tears streamed down every face in that crowd. The audience was worked into a senseless state of ecstasy. When the show reached an appropriate stopping point, we quickly took our bow and exited, pulling the curtain before our daughter could cause any more harm. The crowd erupted into cheers that sounded more like a chorus of ecstatic sobs.

When we walked backstage, the staff was passing around my still-masked daughter, smothering her with hugs and gesticulating their adoration. We could not reveal the nature of the mask to our staff, and so, still yet, we could but stand there helplessly, attempting to conceal our impotence and humiliation. We had lost a battle we had not known we were fighting, and our small daughter stood sneering and victorious.

The next day, the collector visited us. He congratulated us, and said that Kailee had proven herself quite worthy, but was angry that we had not waited a bit longer, as he had asked, so that he might better prepare. Still, he said, the night had been a success, and it was time to start planning the next phase—whatever that meant. To us, after the night we had experienced, those words were terrifying.

He ordered that we call a staff meeting in the wardrobe room as a pretense to clear the halls, and by the time we emerged, the collector and the mask were gone.

He returned the following week and congratulated me again, though I knew not yet for what. He said that the mask, for now, had been hidden in a secret place under the cellar, and that it was time he revealed some truths to me that had thus far been concealed.

That was when he told me of these catacombs beneath us. How he knew they were there, I do not know, but the catacombs, he said, belonged to the Forsworn. It was time, he informed me, that their plans for the catacombs move forward. There had, he told me, been two entrances to this place, just outside of the city. These, he said, had been destroyed just this day, to prevent anyone outside of the organization from finding them.

The highest point in the catacombs was just under this theater, which is why this building had been chosen by his organization. This cellar would become the one, solitary entrance to the vast network of tunnels below.

A team came in the following day, and they dug. They built the trapdoor I now sit on, and they gave me a cheap rug with which to hide it. His people warned me that if anyone ever found it, they would make us suffer. If I ever stole anything from down there, they would make us suffer. If I ever obstructed the members of their upper ranks from coming and going, I would suffer. Access was authorized through a series of questions and answers that had to be precisely asked and answered. I was made to accept several of their members into my troupe—

inexperienced actors who, although they were competent enough and did get better, still confused the existing actors.

Of course, I was not given a choice in any of this. He promoted me to Chair of the Borden Division of the Forsworn—a position, by the way, of no actual power or authority—and made the large antechamber below their meeting place. Sometimes, we all meet down there to discuss plans around the theater that involve me. Most times, however, they meet while I stand watch in this very chair I now sit. Sometimes they take artifacts out, and other times they bring new ones in.

Meanwhile, my daughter stewed with barely contained rage. And she plotted. She had been given a taste of the mask's power, and then it had been stripped from her. I was told by the collector that she was to be given the mask again, at a preordained time, but I did not tell her this. The effects of the mask remained, but just as with my wife, they lessened with time—a fact that further angered her. I believe her anger also had something to do with her diminishing power.

Soon, she discovered her inability to leave, after several attempts in which she was rendered unconscious and unceremoniously dumped back in this very cellar, gagged and trapped inside a wine barrel. As time passed, I believe she decided she'd rather not leave—not without the mask. So she plotted, and I know she plotted, because I watched her. She's clever, but so am I. She had no idea I was undermining her plots, even as she created them. I had things under control...until you came.

You provided us both with an opportunity. I could see in her eyes a fascination. Don't ask me how you did it, my boy, but she was positively smitten. With you, with your mentor, and with your way of life. I'm sure she's sincere about wanting to join you on the road, although I imagine she would grow tired of it quickly and set her sights on much higher aspirations. Still, she does rather like you.

You inspired her. You showed her that there could be a life for her on the outside. You gave her the taste she needed to finally make a brazen attempt at the mask.

But despite the truth of her fondness for you, don't mistake it for love. For feeling love, I'm afraid, she's incapable. You've been manipulated, my boy, and you must now accept this fact. Not that your acceptance much matters right now. What does matter is that you've attracted the eyes of the Sworn, and if you want to protect yourself and those you care about, you must do as I say. They know of you now, and they're watching us all.

We're all playing roles in a production begun many millennia ago. The Sworn are a group privy to secrets of old, and I'm afraid that they intend to do something horrible. I know but little of their plans, but this one thing I know: they plot the resurrection of something long deceased—something likely best left dead—and are getting close to the means to accomplish it. Whatever or whoever it is they intend to resurrect, it will change the face of our world forever.

I know something of your story, Toryn. I know your home was invaded by the Fey. I know you're aware that they've come from some other world. I know you understand that some are intelligent and benevolent, while others are hungry for flesh. They are much like the diverse bunch of creatures who already inhabited this world, except often with powers we don't much understand.

All I've gleaned from the bits of conversation and eavesdropping I've been afforded is that the Fey inhabited this world long ago, but were banished, and now they return. Many, however, are still trapped. For all I know, some of them may be content just where they are. But others are apparently desperate to return here to Uteria.

The Sworn are bent on aiding in the return of one such being. I know naught of his identity, but from what bits I've gathered, his return would be unfortunate, and perhaps even cataclysmic.

I would see them fail at this, Toryn, but I know not how to fight them. Their fingers are in every level of government in every major city. Their spies are everywhere, and little happens without their notice. Organizing against them would be futile, so my only weapon is my cleverness.

So I want you to take this mask. Wear it, Toryn. Use it. You are an empath, like my wife. It's why my daughter was drawn to you, and it's why I'm trusting you now. Take the mask, and find your old mentor. You're going to need support.

After you've found Ehrin, disguise yourselves. You'll be able to affect people's minds—use that. Gather followers. Build your own network of spies and put them to work. Have them infiltrate the Sworn. It's our only chance at stopping them.

CHAPTER 9

I don't know why I believed him. Perhaps it was the way his eyes showed love for his daughter, even as he spoke of her plots against him. Whatever the cause, I did believe him—at least about the imperative to stop the Sworn. It did nothing to lessen my affections for Kailee, but I knew I had no choice. I had to escape, and I had to go alone.

But when I started to move, I found that I was unable. Over the course of Mirkai's story, Kailee had been calling to me, beckoning me. At first, I was able to simply stay focused on Mirkai's words, but by the end of his story, I was positively struggling to hold myself in the chair. Now, in the ensuing silence, her voice came to me: "Toryn, please. Open the door."

Without thought, I was out of the chair and gripping the chain that held the door to its latch. A foot struck me across the face in the spot that was already bruised, and I found myself shaking off the mist of impact. Immediately, I was crawling back toward the trapdoor.

"Toryn, let me out."

My hand was back on the chain. Again, I was struck, but only enough to wrest my hands from the chain. Mirkai's hands roughly gripped my shoulders and pulled me to my feet. "Listen to me, Toryn. You have to resist this. You have to run."

"Bring me the mask, Toryn, and I'll get us out of this," her voice came to me.

I held the mask up and looked at it, then back down at the trapdoor, then at the man blocking my way. Then I noticed the sword resting now next to his seat.

"Toryn, resist." He shook me, but I was lost.

Suddenly, his hand was on the mask, and he pushed it toward me until it was securely on my face.

Instantly, there was silence. Not in the room, but in my head. It was as if I had awoken from a dizzying dream. In my sudden clarity, Kailee's voice still beckoned, but was now faint and outside of my head, barely audible through the thick wood.

My eyes met Mirkai's, and I knew that he had told

me the truth. I pulled the mask from my face, stuffed it into a bag, and walked to the door. Without turning to say goodbye, I left the cellar, and then the theater, and then the city.

It was time to find Ehren, and then to begin.

ABOUT THE AUTHOR

Dane Clark Collins is a writer of fantasy, science fiction, and the occasional nonfiction currently living in the Greater Philadelphia area. He is a lifelong student of philosophy, physics, and all manner of strange and esoteric nonsense, and brings all of this background into his writing.

Dane has been a musician since he was given his first guitar at the age of 10, and some of his work can be found on his web site. He finds his own music quite enjoyable, as he is very narcissistic.

Besides that, he enjoys sushi, has three spoiled dogs, builds his own web sites, reads for two out of three hours of the day, plans to open a dog shelter, and many other things that his readers are dying to know.

Follow Dane at his website and social media:

Website: www.daneclarkcollins.com
Amazon: www.amazon.com/author/daneclarkcollins
Goodreads: www.goodreads.com/danecollins
Twitter: www.twitter.com/dane_collins